UNSINKABLE!

THE CORNER KIDS

Written by Larry Dane Brimner • Illustrated by Christine Tripp

SCHOLASTIC INC.

New York Toronto London Auckland Sydney
Mexico City New Delhi Hong Kong Buenos Aires

For Amanda and Jillian O'Karma
—L.D.B.

For my mother
—C.T.

Reading Consultants
Linda Cornwell
Literacy Specialist

Katharine A. Kane
Education Consultant
(Retired, San Diego County Office of Education and San Diego State University)

ISBN 0-516-24556-2

12 11 10 9 8 7 6 5 4 3 2 1   3 4 5 6 7 8/0

Printed in the U.S.A.   61

First Scholastic printing, April 2003

This book is about **perseverance**.

Alex looked at Gabby's badge.
He looked at Three J's badge.
The badges said "Unsinkable!"

"Those are so cool," he said. Then
he looked at the swimming pool.
"I don't think I'll ever get one."

"Sure you will," said Gabby.

"Just try," said Three J. "The Corner Kids always try." The three friends called themselves the Corner Kids because they lived on opposite corners of the same street.

Alex tried to smile. Gabby and Three J were great swimmers. They could swim from one end of the pool to the other without stopping. Alex didn't think he would ever be able to swim that far. He would never have a badge of his own.

9

Just then, Coach Kim blew her whistle. She held up a bag of badges.

"Who's ready to try for a badge?" she asked.

Alex stepped back, but Gabby and Three J had a different idea.

"Alex is ready," said Gabby.

Before he knew it, Alex was in the pool.

He paddled and he kicked. Then he stopped to catch his breath. He was a long, long way from the other end of the pool.

Alex crawled out of the water.

"Good try," said Coach Kim.
"Who's next?"

The next day and the next, Alex tried again. Each time, he was too tired to make it all the way to the end. It was hard just to make it to the middle.

"I'm quitting," he told Gabby and Three J the next time the Corner Kids came to the pool. "Who needs a silly old badge anyway?"

"You can't quit," said Gabby.

"The Corner Kids never quit," said Three J.

Alex sighed. *I can't do it*, he thought.

He jumped in the pool anyway.

Before long, he was at the middle of the pool.

Then he was farther than he'd ever swum.

Alex paddled and kicked as hard as he could.

"Great job!" said Coach Kim when Alex got to the end of the pool. She gave him a badge.

Alex looked at it. Then he smiled the biggest of smiles. "I'm unsinkable!" he said.

Everyone agreed.

ABOUT THE AUTHOR

Larry Dane Brimner studied literature and writing at San Diego State University and taught school for twenty years. The author of more than seventy-five books for children, many of them Children's Press titles, he enjoys meeting young readers and writers when he isn't at his computer.

ABOUT THE ILLUSTRATOR

Christine Tripp lives in Ottawa, Canada, with her husband Don; four grown children—Elizabeth, Erin, Emily, and Eric; son-in-law Jason; grandsons Brandon and Kobe; four cats; and one very large, scruffy puppy named Jake.